Dec. 2017

D1267341

To my brothers, Stephan and Oliver Nataf,
for their courage and joy in always being themselves!
and to our parents for loving us that way!
-S.N.

For Mom and Dad!
-E.L.

Copyright @ 2016 by Shannon Nataf

First edition 2017

Library of Congress Catalog Card Number 3693419791
ISBN 978-0-692-74264-8

Printed in the USA / bosslitho.com

This book was typeset in Archer
Illustrations were created in watercolor, colored pencil and pen

justbeeplanet.com

Just
Bee

Shannon Nataf

Illustrated by

Echo Li

There was a boy,
he was *little* and *fast*.

But when teams were drawn...

he was always picked last.

One day while standing beside,
  another boy who was boasting with pride

"I am the **BEST**
the best that could be!
OH don't you WISH

*don't you wish
you were ME?!?"*

The little boy slumped,
and looked to the floor.
*"I don't want to be me!*
No, not anymore"

He began wishing,
wishing away
wishing he could be
**DIFFERENT**

even just
for a day.

If only I were SMALLER
I would *run* through their knees.

If I were only
BIGGER

I could *jump*
over trees.

If I were only
**COLDER**
I could make
*everything* freeze.

If only
I were OLDER
they would *have*
to say please.

If I were only
STRONGER
I could lift
the *whole* park.

If I could catch *all* the **LIGHT**

they'd have to play in the dark.

In that very moment
the boy heard a small sound.
A BUZZ started buzzing
but was *nowhere* to be found.

He peered **UP** over head
and searched **DOWN** below.

**WHERE** could
the noise be from?

BUZZING BUZZING BUZZING BUZZING BUZZING BUZZING BUZZING BUZZING BUZZING BUZZING BUZZING BUZZING BUZZING BUZZING BUZZING BUZZING BUZZING BUZZING BUZZING BUZZING BUZZING BUZZING BUZZING BUZZING BUZZING BUZZING BUZZING BUZZING BUZZING BUZZING BUZZING BUZZING BUZZING

He *really*
    didn't know!!!

BUZZING BUZZING BUZZING BUZZING BUZZING BUZZING BUZZING BUZZING BUZZING BUZZING BUZZING BUZZING BUZZING BUZZING BUZZING BUZZING BUZZING BUZZING BUZZING BUZZING

BUZZING BUZZING BUZZING BUZZING BUZZING BUZZING BUZZING BUZZING BUZZING BUZZING BUZZING BUZZING BUZZING

Then he saw it
right in front of his nose
   a BEE was following
wherever he goes.

"HEY YOU!" said the bee
   "I—AM—ME

If I were *any* other
I would be eeeZzy to see."

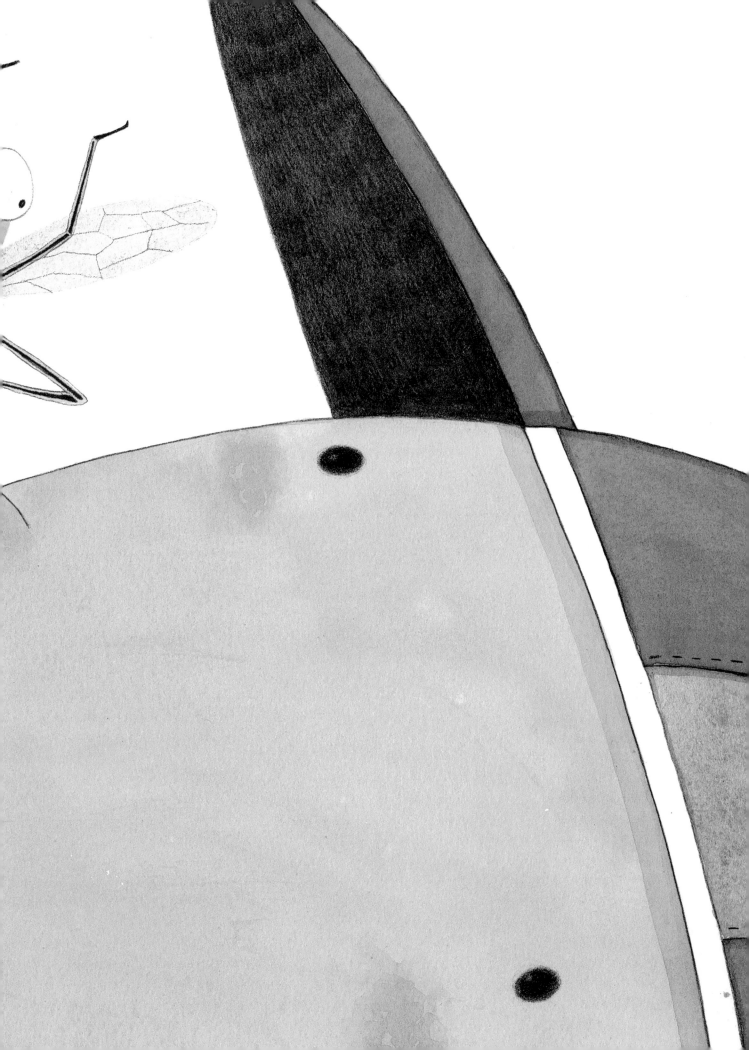

"A Zebra has stripes
and Zzey look quite nice.
But I CAN make honey
and Zzzats Pretty Sweet!!

I *couldn't* do it
if I had Zzzebra feet!"

"Take a ChimpanZZzee"
    said zee Bee
        "Zzey eat bananazZ
    and can climb
    in the trees
        but Zzey can't
    do Zissss..."

And he
started to
swiishhh.

BUZZING BUZZI

BUZZING BUZZING BUZZING BUZZ

BUZZING BUZZING BUZZING BUZZI

G BUZZING BUZZING BUZZING BUZZI

Flying *FAST*
through the air,
without even a care.

He did **BACK** flips
and **FRONT** flips

with *zig zagging* flair!

"HOW about a *FISH*"
said the boy.
"Don't you ever *WISH*
you were a fish!?!"

"oh **I DID**, I did
how I *wisssshed* I were a **FISH**!!!

ZZzey swim in Zze Sea
and play in Zze waves
I dream't I was a fish
for *so many dayz.*"

"BUT Zzen I discovered
   Zzat Zzey don't have flowers!
Just Zze thought of it
   and I smelled flowers for *hours*!"

"So you see" said the Bee.
   "I like being me.
There are things I can't do
   but I DO what I CAN!
I do my BEST with all that **I AM!**"

"It ALL works together
you *must* understand.
If the WHOLE world were elephants
there'd be no place to stand!!!"

"The world NEEDS you
to be **YOU** can't you see?!
They'll never be another
who can BEE all you can BE!"

"OH, I SEE!" said the boy
"I'm the **ME-ist** of Me
**I AM** something
only I can be.

Others might try
and try with great might
but no matter the effort
they couldn't be **ME** just right!"

"I am the way
    that I SING
without any fright,

and the way
    that I FEEL
when I'm tucked
    in at night.

I am the way
   that I **LEAP**
without even a blink,

and **ALL** of the

Amazing things that I **THINK**."

The boy started smiling.
He **GOT IT** for SURE.
He never wished to be another.
NO, not anymore!

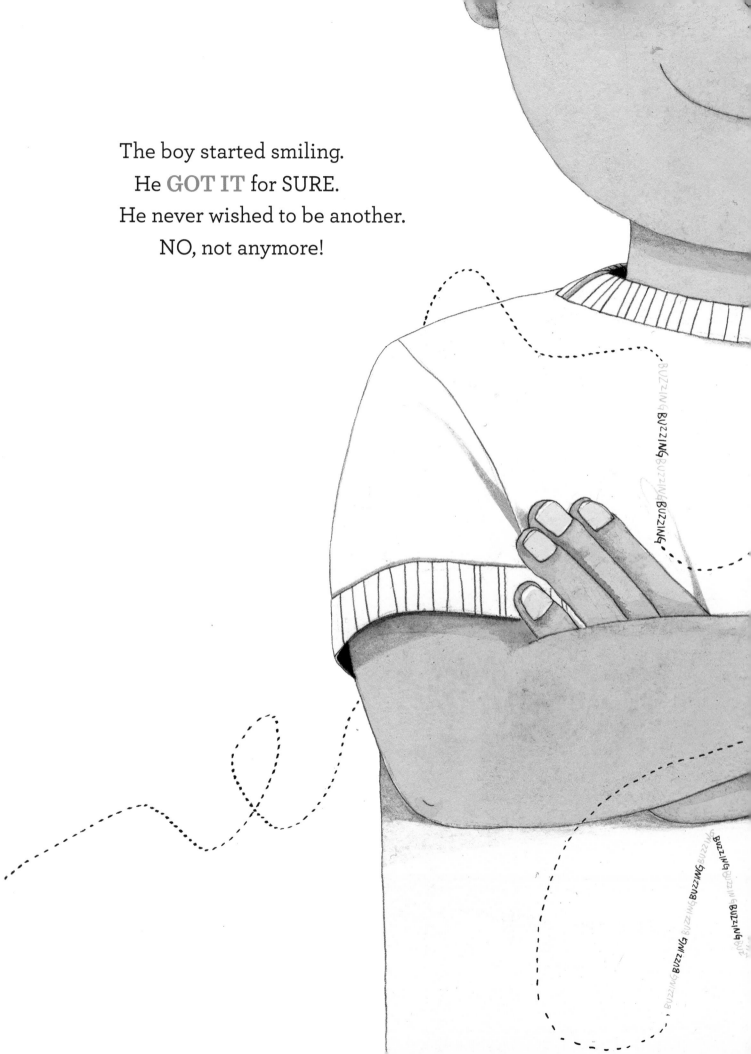

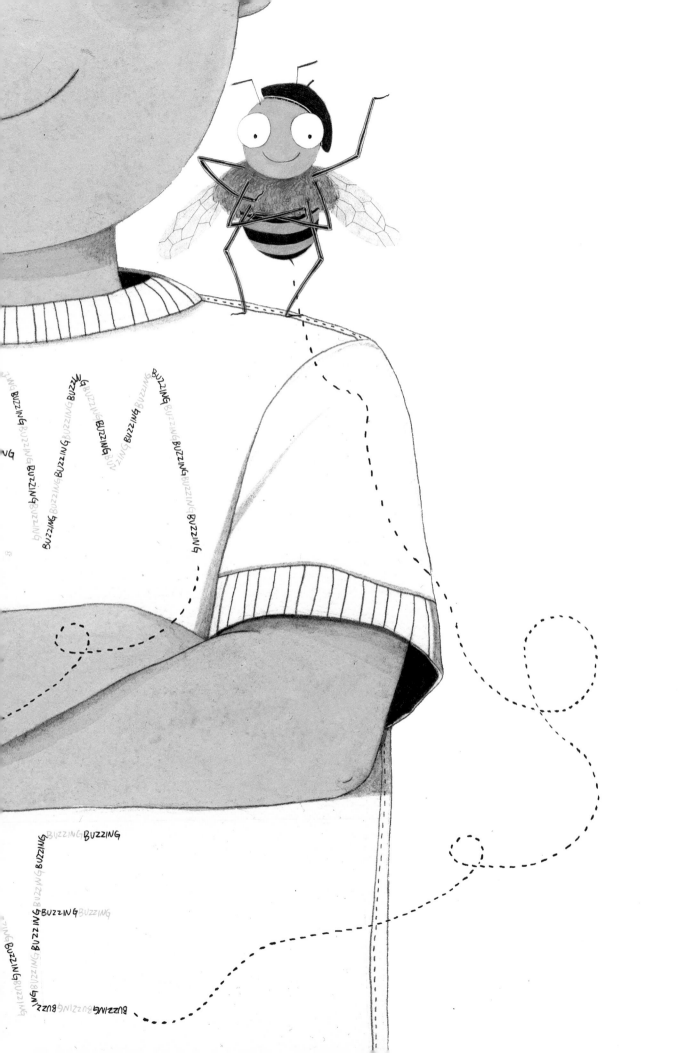

From that day forward
   he was HAPPY as could be.
     Filled with *WONDER* and *CURIOSITY*!

   Of who he was
     and the things he could do...

...and NOW its your turn,

to **ENJOY**
*being YOU!*

BUZZING BUZZING BUZZING BUZZING

BUZZING BUZZING BUZZING

So many AmazZing reasons
I LOVE BEE-ing ME!
Here are just a few
for us to see...

1. _____

2. _____

3. _____

4. _____

List four things you LOVE about who you are

# This is me!

**is**

Draw a picture of you doing something that makes you HAPPY

My Name is:

Age: